Ask Mia

by Iris Hudson
Illustrated by Blanche Sims

Kane Press, Inc.
New York

For Barbara Van Riper Cossman
—I.H.
For Dr. Jerry and Sandy Greenberg,
with appreciation   *—Blanche*

Book Design/Art Direction: Roberta Pressel

Text copyright © 2006 by Iris Hudson
Illustrations copyright © 2006 by Blanche Sims

Library of Congress Cataloging-in-Publication Data

Hudson, Iris.
    Ask Mia / by Iris Hudson; illustrated by Blanche Sims.
      p. cm. — (Math matters.)
    Summary: When Bossy Mia starts a newspaper, she refuses to publish Amy's survey results unless they are in pictograph form, which challenges Amy's math skills as well as their friendship.
    ISBN 1-57565-188-2 (alk. paper)
    [1. Newspapers—Fiction. 2. Graphic methods—Fiction. 3. Surveys—Fiction.
4. Schools—Fiction. 5. Friendship—Fiction.]
    I. Sims, Blanche, ill. II. Title. III. Series.
    PZ7.H86646Ask 2006
    [E]—dc22
    2006003546

                                                                      CIP
                                                                             AC

10 9 8 7 6 5 4 3 2 1

First published in the United States of America in 2006 by Kane Press, Inc.
Printed in Hong Kong.

MATH MATTERS is a registered trademark of Kane Press, Inc.

www.kanepress.com

"I'm going to meet with Mr. Albee about starting a newspaper," Mia said. "You in?"

"Sure!" I told her.

"But Amy," said Mia, *"I'll* do the talking."

Mia likes to do things her way.

And her way works—most of the time.

Mr. Albee listened while Mia talked. And talked. "A newspaper will help with math, science, and reading. So puh-*leeeaze!* Can we do it? Can we? Pleasepleaseplease?"

Mr. Albee smiled. "Okay, okay—I give in!"

"Thanks, Mr. A!" Mia said. She winked at me. Mia does make things happen!

"So Amy, do you want to be the photographer?" Mia handed me her digital camera. "You can use this."

"Cool!" I said. "Can I also be a reporter?"

"Come to the meeting," said Mia. "We'll talk."

"We'll talk" means no. But oh, so what. It would be fun using Mia's camera.

Ella, Luis, and Joey were at the meeting, too. "What should we put in the paper?" Ella asked.

"Jokes!" Luis said. "Kids can send them in."

"Mmmm, not sure," said Mia. "I've already asked kids to send in letters to Ask Mia."

"What is *that?*" said Ella.

"My advice column!" Mia replied. "I'm telling kids how to solve their problems."

"Do kids even want advice?" Ella asked.

Mia raised an eyebrow. "Of course."

"Of course *not!*" said Luis. "Kids want jokes and quizzes. Like, 'If a hen-and-a-half lays an egg-and-a-half in a day-and-a-half, then how many—'"

"T-t-t-t," interrupted Mia. "That's worse than woodchucks chucking wood."

Joey jumped up. "Woodchucks! How about a wildlife column? Today I saw a mallard duck sitting in a puddle on the soccer field, and—"

"That duck is a dope," said Mia. "I threw it a potato chip, and it ran into the bushes."

"Maybe it's building a nest!" said Joey.

Mia stared at him. "On the soccer field?"

Joey slumped back into his chair.

"*Actually,*" I said. "I like jokes. Wildlife, too."

Mia looked at me. "So do I. That's why I'm writing my Wild About Ponies story."

"Starring your pony—as *wildlife?*" Luis asked.

"Correct."

Gosh, I thought. That was a stretch.

Mia put on a visor. "I've got a lot to do. When I'm wearing this, no one talks."

The room grew quiet. "The meeting's over?" asked Luis. Mia pointed to her visor.

"We're not finished," Ella said. "I want to write a sports column—with interviews!"

"It's already done," said Mia. "Mia the Cowgirl."

Ella blinked. "You interviewed *yourself?*"

"For the *sports column?*" Luis asked.

"Yup," Mia said. "Gotta go now! Buh-bye!"

We followed Mia outside. "Stop!" Ella called.
"Let's find out what kids really want to read!"

"I'll bet it's not Mia and more Mia," Luis said.

"Why don't we ask around?" said Joey.

"Yes—take a survey!" I gave him a thumbs-up.

"Fine," said Mia. "Start tomorrow. I'll put
your results in the paper. Amy can take photos."

That sounded like fun!

The next morning, Mia waved a handful of letters at me. "Read these. Wait until you see how good my advice is."

"You already started?" I asked. "What about the survey? What if no one wants an advice column?"

"*Everyone* will want it," said Mia. She gave me the letters.

Dear Mia,
  Someone I know is a ball hog. How can I make her be a better team player?
                    Left Out

Dear Left Out,
  Be a winner, not a whiner. Learn to play better. Then maybe she'll pass you the ball.
                    Mia

Dear Mia,
  When I can't figure out math problems I freak out and give up. I just don't get it.
                    Help!

Dear Help,
  Quitters are losers. There's a solution to every problem. Have you read your math book lately?
                    Mia

Dear Mia,
  I really want a goat but my mom says no.
                    Petless

Dear Petless,
  Make a chart showing reasons for having a goat, and name the goat after your mother. That's how I got my pony.
                    Mia

13

I looked at Mia. "You really think Petless's mom would want a goat named after her?"

"Why not? Wouldn't you?"

"No. And to be honest, you and your pony don't belong in Wildlife—or Sports."

Mia grabbed the letters back. "Yes, we do!"

Hmm, I thought. We'll see about *that*.

The survey began at morning recess.

"Would you like a sports column in our newspaper?" Ella asked Tanya. "Featuring pony riding, maybe?"

"No. Featuring *soccer,*" she said.

"Do you like advice columns?" asked Luis.

"No, I don't."

Click! I took Tanya's picture.

"Sam, you like to read about wildlife,
right?" Luis asked. "Like ponies, for example?"

"Ponies, no," replied Sam. "Mallards, yes."

"Would you read an advice column written
by Mia?" Ella asked.

Sam made a face. "Why would I need advice
from Mia?"

I snapped his picture.

"Hey, Lily?" Ella asked. "Think you'd read a column where Mia tells you what to do?"

"I'd rather read jokes." Lily started to giggle. "Listen to this one!"

"We're kind of in a hurry here," said Ella.

"A duck walks into a store—" Lily began.

I took her picture as Ella pulled me away.

"But what about the punch line?" Lily called.

"See, Mia?" Luis said after recess. "Kids like jokes and sports and wildlife—*not* advice."

Mia rolled her eyes. "You only interviewed *three* kids! That doesn't prove anything."

I had to admit, she was right.

"If you want to do a survey, talk to a hundred kids!" Mia told us. "Then make a pictograph. Any questions?"

"Yeah," said Luis. "What's a pictograph?"

"Don't Ask Mia," Mia said, and walked off.

"Ask me!" I said.
"I know. Well, sort of.
A pictograph is a graph
with pictures."

I drew one for them.

"Ah!" said Ella. "I get
it—I think."

FAVORITE SEASON	
Spring	👤👤👤
Summer	👤👤👤👤
Fall	👤👤
Winter	👤

So we surveyed.
And surveyed. And surveyed.

20

Later we went to Ella's house to make
our pictograph.

"My hand is so tired," grumbled Luis.

"Mine, too," said Joey. "I'm sick, sick,
sick of stick people!"

"We're almost done," I told them.

Ella sighed. "I'll get more paper."

The next morning we marched up to Mia.

"We surveyed a hundred kids," Ella began. She and Joey unrolled the graph.

"*Tada!*" said Luis. "Forty for jokes and quizzes, thirty for wildlife, twenty for sports, and only ten for advice!"

He did a victory dance.

I could tell Mia was miffed, but she was trying not to show it. "Sorry, guys," she said. "This is way too big to fit in the paper."

"You're just mad because you don't like the way the survey came out," said Ella.

On went the visor. Mia scuttled back into the library.

"I give up," Joey said.

"Me, too," said Ella. "I hate the newspaper."

"Let's be winners, not whiners!" I told them. "We can figure this out!"

"Leave us alone," said Luis. "We all quit."

Okay, I thought. It was time for Mia to listen to *me* for a change.

I stormed inside.

"Take that off," I demanded.

Mia held onto her visor with both hands.

"You say every problem has a solution," I said. "Why don't you help us find one?"

"I'm busy," Mia told me crisply.

"And bossy! The other kids are quitting. And so am I."

Later I found a note in my cubby.

I wrote back.

Dear Amy,
    I feel like I always have to be the star. It ruins my friendships. Any advice?
                    Mia
P.S. Want to make a pictograph smaller? Let each stick figure stand for more than one vote.

Dear Mia,
    My advice? Be a star—but let others shine, too.
                    Amy
P.S. Thanks for the pictograph tip.

I hurried outside. "Hey, guys! Our problem is solved." I told everyone about Mia's tip.

"How does that help us?" asked Joey.

"Think about it," I said. "Jokes and quizzes got forty votes. So if we make one stick person stand for ten votes . . ."

"Then four stick people will stand for forty votes," Luis said. "And the pictograph will fit!"

Every pictograph has a sentence that tells you how many items each symbol stands for. It's called the **key**. Example: Each 🧍 stands for ten votes.

The next day, I gave Mia our new pictograph.
"Mm hm," she said. "I can print this."

"On the front page? With jokes and quizzes?"

"Oh, why not?" said Mia. "But you really
want a wildlife story about a dizzy duck?
Instead of a prancing pony?"

"Yup. You can still do an advice column,
though." I winked at her. "If you keep it short."

"Why don't the two of us share the advice column?" Mia asked. "We can be partners."

"*Equal* partners?"

"Totally," said Mia. "So, how about it, Amy? Pleasepleaseplease? Puh-*leeeaze?*"

I covered my ears and laughed. "Okay, okay!"

We ran outside to find the other kids.

"Hey, Joey!" called Mia. "Take our picture!
Oops, I mean—will you *please* take our picture?"

Mia and I slung our arms around each other's
shoulders and smiled for the camera.

Amy and Mia, I thought. We were ready to
make things happen!

SPORTS
Tanya Gets Going — by Ella

She shoots! She scores! Tanya, our very own school superstar, made the winning goal at Friday's soccer game. "It was awe

photo by Amy

best sport."
the coach
free kick
amazing!
charged
goalie
ran to
faked
net
won!

KIDS' REPORTER
News by Kids—for Kids!

YOU ASKED FOR IT!

We surveyed one hundred kids to find out what you want to read about, and here's what you said!

THINGS YOU LIKE TO READ ABOUT MOST	
Sports	👤👤
Wildlife	👤👤👤
Jokes & Quizzes	👤👤👤👤
Advice	👤

Each 👤 stands for 10 votes.

JOKES & QUIZZES
You Quack Me Up!

A duck walks into a store and says, "Lipstick, please."

The cashier says, "Are you going to pay for it?"

The duck answers, "Put it on my bill."

—sent in by Lily
photo by Amy

Luis's Quiz

Question: If a hen-and-a-half lays an egg-and-a-half in a day-and-a-half, how many eggs does one hen lay in one day?

Answer: one egg

WILDLIFE
Quackerrific by Joey

Do you like mallards?
My friend Sam does.
He spotted one on the
soccer field last week.
Male mallards are
colorful, but are lousy
quackers. The females
are excellent quacker
but are plain-lookin

Sam gets wild, photo by Amy

Mallards like water.
They eat seeds, worms,
berries, smallish fish,
potato chips. A
lard's life

ADVICE
Ask Amy & Mia

Amy and Mia, photo by Joey

Dear Amy & Mia,
When I can't figure out
math problems I freak
out and give up. I just
don't get it.
Help!

Dear Help,
How about trying
the after-school
tutoring program?
It works!
Amy & Mia

Dear Amy & Mia,
I really want a goat but
my mom says no.
Petless

Dear Petless,
Ask for a cat. At least
you can snuggle with it!
Amy & Mia

Dear Amy & Mia,
Someone I know is a ball
hog. How can I make her
be a better team player?
Left Out

Dear Left Out,
Write her a note and
tell her how you feel.
Amy & Mia
P.S. Be honest.

PICTOGRAPHS

Look at the pictograph. What information do you see?

Favorite DVD						
Cartoon	💿	💿	💿	💿	💿	💿
Comedy	💿	💿	💿	💿		
Mystery	💿	💿				
Wildlife	💿	💿	💿	💿		

2 + 2 + 2 + 2 + 2 + 2 = 12 votes

2 + 2 + 2 + 2 = 8 votes

2 + 2 = 4 votes

2 + 2 + 2 + 2 = 8 votes

Each 💿 stands for 2 votes.

What happens if you let 💿 stand for a different number of votes?

Favorite DVD			
Cartoon	💿	💿	💿
Comedy	💿	💿	
Mystery	💿		
Wildlife	💿	💿	

4 + 4 + 4 = 12 votes

4 + 4 = 8 votes

4 = 4 votes

4 + 4 = 8 votes

Each 💿 stands for 4 votes.

Why might you also need a half symbol?

Think: Half of 8 = 4
          Half of 💿 = ◖

Favorite DVD		
Cartoon	💿	◖
Comedy	💿	
Mystery	◖	
Wildlife	💿	

8 + 4 = 12 votes

8 = 8 votes

4 = 4 votes

8 = 8 votes

Each 💿 stands for 8 votes.